IMOGENE'S ANTLERS

IMOGENE'S ANTLERS
By David Small

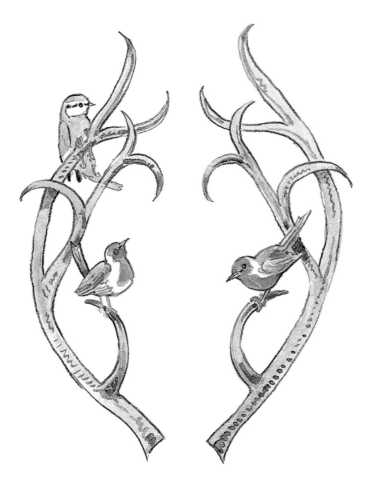

Dragonfly Books —— New York

All rights reserved. Published in the United States by Dragonfly Books, an
imprint of Random House Children's Books, a division of Random House,
Inc., New York. Originally published in hardcover in the United States by
Crown Publishers, an imprint of Random House Children's Books, in 1985.

Dragonfly Books with the colophon
is a registered trademark of Random House, Inc.

Visit us on the Web! www.randomhouse.com/kids

Educators and librarians, for a variety of teaching tools,
visit us at www.randomhouse.com/teachers

The Library of Congress has cataloged the hardcover edition of this work
as follows:

Small, David.
Imogene's antlers.
Summary: One Thursday Imogene wakes up with a pair of antlers growing
out of her head and causes a sensation wherever she goes.
ISBN 978-0-375-81048-0 (trade) — ISBN 978-0-375-91048-7 (lib. bdg.)
— ISBN 978-0-517-56242-0 (pbk.)
1. Children's stories, American. [1. Humorous stories] I. Title.
PZ7.S638Im 1985 [E]   84012085

MANUFACTURED IN CHINA

48 47 46 45 44 43 42

On Thursday, when Imogene
woke up, she found she
had grown antlers.

Getting dressed was difficult,

and going through a door
now took some thinking.

Imogene started down
for breakfast…

but got
hung up.

"OH !!"
Imogene's mother
fainted away.

The doctor poked, and prodded, and scratched his chin.

He could find nothing wrong.

The school principal
glared at Imogene
but had no advice to
offer.

Her brother, Norman, consulted
the encyclopedia, and then announced
that Imogene had turned into a rare
form of miniature elk!

Imogene's mother fainted again
and was carried upstairs to bed.

Imogene went into the kitchen.
Lucy, the kitchen maid, had her
sit by the oven to dry some towels.
"Lovely antlers," said Lucy.

The cook, Mrs. Perkins, gave
Imogene a doughnut, then
decked her out with several more
and sent her into the garden
to feed the birds.

"You'll be lots of fun
to decorate,
come Christmas!"
said Mrs. Perkins.

Later, Imogene wandered upstairs.
She found the whole family
in Mother's bedroom.

"Doughnuts anyone?" she asked.

Her mother said, "Imogene, we have
decided there is only one thing to do.
We must hide your antlers
under a hat!"

Norman telephoned
the milliner.

At three o'clock
the milliner
arrived.

Rapidly
he sketched
a few designs,

then set to work.

"*Voilà!*"
said the
milliner.

"*Bravo!*
Bravissimo!"
cried his
assistants.

THUD!
Imogene's mother
had to be carried away
once more.

After dinner,
Imogene practiced
her piano
lesson.

Then, yawning,
she folded her music…

kissed the family…

and went to bed.

Imogene sighed,
remembering the long,
eventful day.

On Friday, when Imogene
woke up, the antlers had disappeared.

When she came down to breakfast, the family was overjoyed to see her back to normal...

until she came into the room.